For my parents.

Acknowledgements

I am deeply indebted to Genevieve Grant. Thank you for your friendship and your masterful editing skills. That thing you do — where you ask the question that lands like a kick to the back of the knee? Amazing! And what's even more amazing is that you're always there to pick me up, dust me off, and point me in the right direction. You've made every page of this book better by half.

Once again I am grateful for my brilliant copyeditor and lifelong friend Ruth Lytle: Your ability to find a grain of salt in a sandbox is only one of your many superpowers. The turtles and I thank you for being so generous with your time. Thanks also for all of the laughter: I'm certain our hyper-specific t-shirt enterprise will keep us giggling for years to come.

Thanks as well to Jenny Jaeckel, co-founder of the Room Six Waterski Club. Our time spent talking about our creative endeavours has helped me so much. We. Are. Killing. It.

It is perplexing how I (a reclusive, daydreaming, card-carrying introvert) have amassed such an extraordinary group of friends. My Victoria crew: Cori, Dave, Lynn, Jelena, Tara, Leigh, JL, Nandi, Jo, Jazmyn, Di, and my Vancouver peeps: Linda, Allison, Andrea, Nicole, Sarah. Thank you all for your kindness and generosity of spirit. My dream of us all ending up in the same old folks home is only growing stronger by the day.

Special thanks to my sensitivity readers Kingsley Strudwick and Glory Wiersema for their insightful feedback. Any mistakes or misrepresentations are my fault alone.

Cori, Kelly, and Heather — my apologies for stealing "Nutmeg" and "Roxy" right out from under you. I'm confident I will be forgiven, because people who name their cars are the best!

Andrea Kucherawy, thank you for making this self-conscious gal feel downright handsome.

Many thanks to the unfailingly supportive and vastly talented Gareth Gaudin.

And last but not least, to my mom and dad and sister and the rest of my wonderful family — your love and support are unparalleled. Thank you for being my soft place to land.

scriiiitch!

Calli?

Time to - Hey! What are you doing?

You don't smoke!

I'm not -

I mean, I won't -

I was just mucking about, feeling sorry for myself

Chin up, doll

It was fun while it lasted

Honestly, I'm a bit relieved to hear that

What do you mean?

I just remember the summer I worked as a bus cleaner: the hyper-macho culture

Oh. Calli. You are such a sensitive soul. But you have to remember, I practically grew up at my dad's shop

I've heard it all, I've seen it all

Believe me — I can handle it

Sure, but then there's that added layer — that other...

I just worry — 'cause you're very open about...

Being trans?

Yeah

Well, I'm not naive enough to say everyone would be cool with it. Victoria sometimes feels pretty progressive, but I know guys like that can be total dicks

It's kind of a contextual thing: If I don't feel it's a safe situation I'd only come out to certain people and not others

Anyway, you don't have to worry. My love for fashion won out

Props to my dad for getting me a sewing machine when I was 12. Not a typical dad move

Your dad sounds amazing

He's the best!

So what about you?

What's the plan?

Not much of one really

Wrap it up, get a regular job

Back to retail?

Yup

I wonder if it'll be hard to go back to working for someone else? You know, after being your own boss

It might be, but I sure won't miss the stress of keeping everything going

Ooh! I can picture you working at that mystery bookshop on Fort Street

Right up your alley.

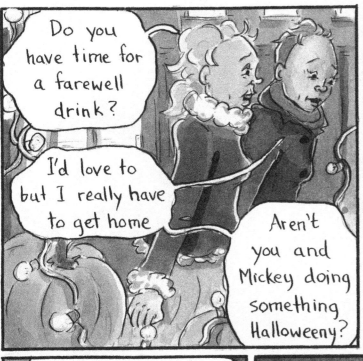

Do you have time for a farewell drink?

I'd love to but I really have to get home

Aren't you and Mickey doing something Halloweeny?

Yes, but only later. I'm actually going to meet some of his friends from Up Island for the first time...

... And he wants me to meet his family next weekend

That's a lot of pressure!

He sounds really into you

I know right !?!

I never thought I'd say this...

... But I feel like he's Too into me!

Like, I wish he'd get a hobby or something

It's suffocating!

Oh, Roxy ... why today, of all days, did you have to pile on?

I am so fucking angry right now!

I knew she would do this. I just knew it!

I knew she would bail on me at the last minute!

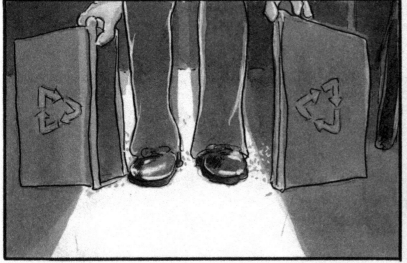

14

Hey,
Nutmeg

15

Oh no

Calli?

Ch-Ch-Chet? Oh, thank God

I forgot I don't have a key for the gate

19

20

It IS a big deal!

And then The Hive

The Hive practically runs itself

I used to hate working from my apartment. By 10 in the morning I would be going stir-crazy being on my own

It was a no-brainer to create a hub for people like me

Your business was a super unique concept

You took a risk

You should be really proud of yourself

Are you going to stay to the 15th? Or all of November?

I don't know yet

I have to come up with rent pronto

I've never not been on time... I have to talk to our landlady

I feel like such a schmuck

Can you borrow it from anyone? Your parents? Your girlfriend, what's-her-name?

I'll punch her in the neck!

Oh my God. That is so sweet

You're adorable. Go on, text her

Done

Here we go

Let me talk to Mrs. Wong. I'm sure I can buy you a few days

Oh, and have you texted Viv to see if her dad's shop can get your car towed?

No, I'll do that

Cheers! To the next chapter

May you one day see the light at the end of the tunnel

And may it not be a train!

Oh great! We'll just have to- Oh, there she is

Calli!

It seems perfect

Ellen, this is Calli, Calli, Ellen

Hello

Hi

Ellen came to The Hive this afternoon to check out one of the workspaces we have advertised

Yes, but I was hoping for an office with an actual door

So I mentioned to Ellen that you had a room upstairs you might be willing to rent -you know- the smaller of your two offices?

Oh right, well-

It would be perfect

Such a charming space!

You've seen it?

I talked Mrs. Wong into giving me a key to show it

Oh... okay

I'll be by tomorrow morning

What just happened?

Did you tell her it was this much? It almost covers my entire rent!

I knew you wouldn't ask for enough

Did you notice her boots? They're worth twice as much as this

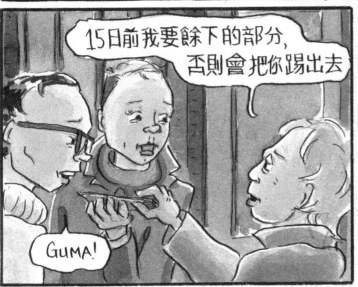

15日前我要餘下的部分，否則會把你踢出去

GUMA!

Brutal! She says the rest is due by the 15th

Easy come, easy go I guess

Guma. Is that Mrs. Wong's first name?

Not exactly, but she'll answer to both

She likes being called that

Smuggling in groceries?

Um...

I take it you're sleeping up there now?

Well, kind of. I figure it's just for the month

Good point. Okay, sure, I'll give it a try. My Visa card could use the help

Oh, Calli don't flirt with credit card debt at a time like this

A trick I learned from an ex-boyfriend is to freeze your credit card

freeze it?

In a block of ice. It doesn't hurt it, and it stops impulse buying cold

"Cold", get it?

Ha! I may have to try that

Good morning, ladies

Hi, Ellen

Hello

I'd better get back to it. Good luck with your book

Thank you, Stephanie

I'm ready to get started

Let's get you set up then

mergow

Oh, Hello!

Just like that

Say, does this work?

It should

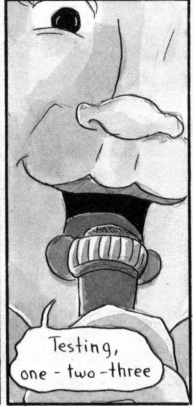

Testing, one - two - three

Click

Testing-one-two-three

Ha!

And the typewriter too?

Yes, it should as well

Do you think I could use this?

Of course

I don't do laptops

I usually write by hand, but it might be fun to try this

Well...

I guess I should quit procrastinating and get to work!

Help yourself to coffee. The bathroom is also just through there

Oh, and I'd better give you a key because I'll be in and out

Why, thank you

Calli?

You won't be offended if I close my door?

I find it so hard to concentrate

pfoomp!

MERGOW!!!

GAH!

You again!

merrrup

No. I'm not going to start feeding you

In fact, you and I need to go on an austerity diet

You, kibble

Me, credit

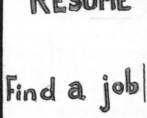

嘿!女偵探

拿著這個

Um...

I guess I'm delivering this?

MING
WONG
Y CLEANER

VISA

5th floor
1875
Douglas

走!

And this must be for me?

Since they paid by VISA

Thank you, Guma

It's paid for

It's a tip

STEVE MAN

Hey! It's Jessica Fletcher

How goes it, Calli?

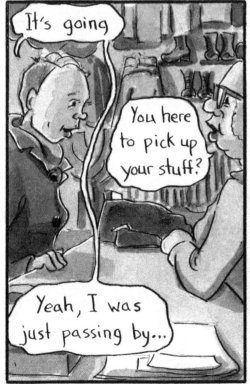

It's going

You here to pick up your stuff?

Yeah, I was just passing by...

I tell ya...

I'm sure going to miss your clients

Bumbling around the store until they had their A-ha moment

You were onto something

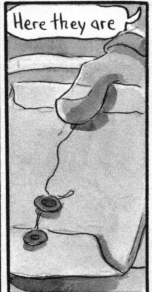

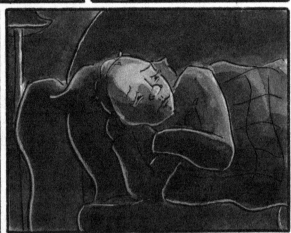

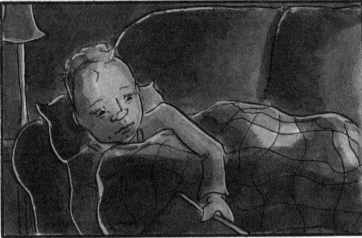

45

Good morning

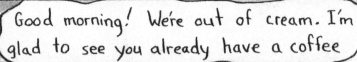

Good morning! We're out of cream. I'm glad to see you already have a coffee

I treated myself to a fancy one today

How's your book coming along?

Oh it's coming. Just chipping away bit by bit

I admire your self-discipline — Working at it every single day

If only self-discipline equalled talent!

Well, I'd better get back to work

55

Wait... is that Tracy's...

Carol...

Oh, God. Why her of all people?

Calli Westbrook?

Yes

Upstairs?

Yes

How's business Sherlock?

So you don't have a picture or her last name or an address, or her husband's name, and you didn't see her get taken

You saw her walking down the alley with a dark haired man and get into a black SUV type vehicle

It wasn't like that... it was more forceful: He was gripping her by the arm, almost dragging her, and it looked like he pushed her into the car

Did she call out?

No...

Okay, well, if she doesn't show up in the next 48 hours, you can file a missing persons report

And a last name would be helpful

GAH!

Jesus Christ, Cat!

You're gonna give me a heart attack one day

How do you manage to sneak in all the time?

Maybe that was her husband, and maybe he had just told her some really bad news...

Maybe he was just helping her to the car

merrqow

I never even asked for her last name

Stupid. Stupid. Stupid

And Carol the cop

She didn't have to be so mean...

She's the one who... who...

SOB

SOB

She's usually here by this time...

Ellen?

Oh, sorry, I thought you were someone else

Can I help you?

Is this the typewriter repair place?

Um, sure

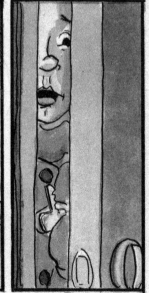

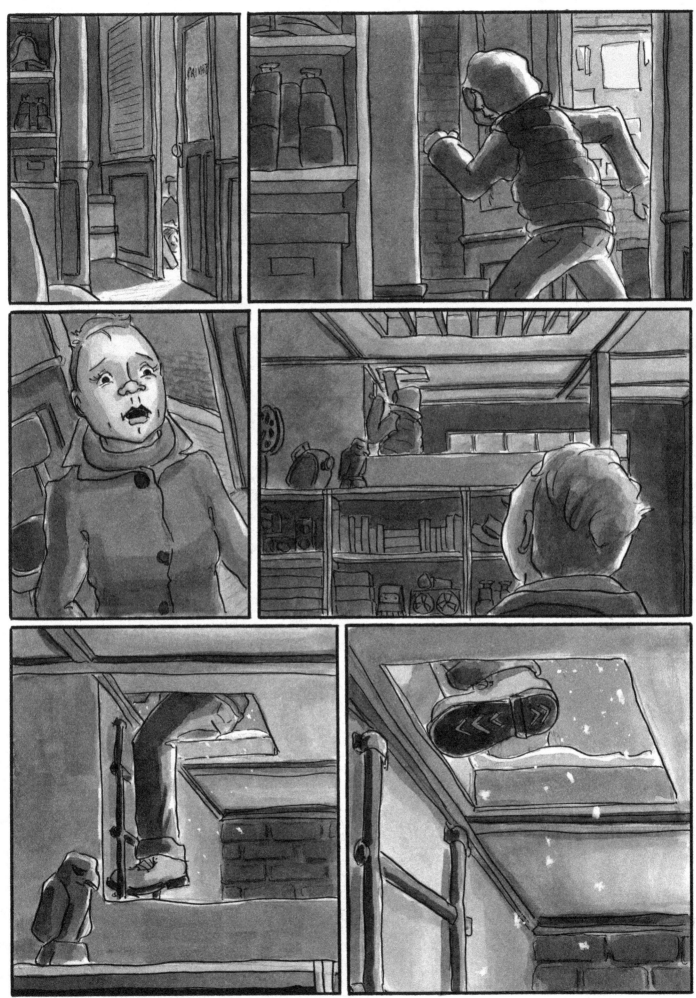

Chapter 6

The Weak and the Wicked

70

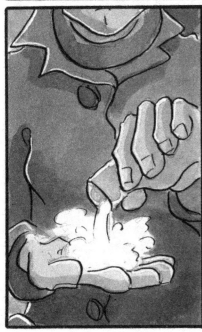

The other day I failed to notice a basket of laundry that "needed" to be folded

You'd think I was ... ah! Never mind

Needless to say, we have different ideas on what's important

Well, if it's important to her maybe

Anyways...

If she seemed extra standoffish tonight it's probably because she resents your freedom, No kids, your own business...

You're living the dream

No, I'm not

What? You're pregnant?

fffoomp

Tracy and I broke up

WHAT!?!

And the business tanked. I closed it down at the end of last month. Now I'm sleeping at the office, and today there was a break-in ...

I couldn't bring myself to stay there tonight

Dude. Why didn't you tell me?

What happened with you and Tracy?

She cheated on me...

You know, I had this fantasy about being a private detective... and there I was, totally clueless about her having an affair

I suck at the one thing I wanted to do the most. What a joke! I'm a complete failure!

Whoa! Touch the brakes a little, Nancy Drew

Calli, You are NOT a failure!

At least you gave it a shot

Dad would've been so proud of you for taking a chance like that

Thanks, Theo

You want to talk about failure...look at me: I never ever play music anymore, and I've got a job I can barely stand

You used to like it though

What happened?

Here is good

Thanks for dropping me off

You sure you don't want me to come up?

Make sure no one is lurking about?

Hey, Calli

No, I'm fine

Hiya!

She's cute

Theo!

What? Too soon?

She's not my type

What?... Attractive? ... Chic? ...Urban?... Feminine?... Asian?... Optically challenged?

You are SUCH a pest! She's straight

I don't waste my time on straight women

Always ends in heartache

Good morning, Guma

What did she say?

Oh, nothing. She's just being a busy body as usual

Mmmmm... this is exactly what I needed. Thanks

Hey, do you have a ballpoint pen in your bag?

I didn't know you were still seeing Charles

I'm not. It's been over for ages

I thought we could try to be friends, but he's not ready

I'm sorry

It's fine. It's just too bad

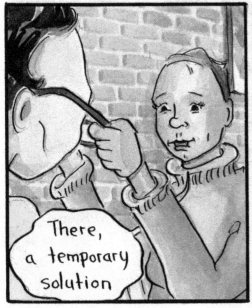

There, a temporary solution

I can see! Thanks MacGyver

Uh-oh

Everything that meant something to me was already at the office

I think on some level I knew we weren't right for each other

I just didn't have the courage to look at that

Why do you always call her "what's-her-name"?

Because whenever she came by she never seemed proud of you

And she SHOULD HAVE been!

Thanks for that, Steph

Anyway...

Ugh! All bills

At least my Visa should be tiny this month

What?

Holy!

There's a $750 charge on here...

There is NO way...

Does what's-her-face ever use your card?

82

Chapter 7

Shadow of a Doubt

Oh, hello

Come on in

You've lost your collar, big guy

Mergow

You look a little naked

Oh, Sammy

Buddy, you're not helping

You are such a stereotype

85

Nope

I think we're done for tonight

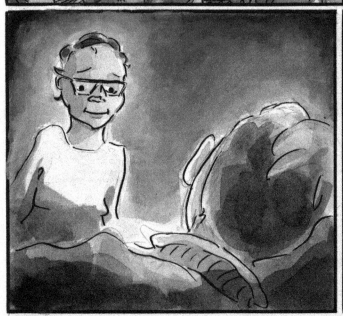

Chroma Industries

Chroma Industries NY, NY. Artisan supplies. Call us for a catalogue. 1-800...

That's disappointingly vague

What a crappy website... no online shopping, no address no hours of operation

New York... three hour time difference-they should be open by now

♪♫♪♫

Speaker

♪♫ – Hello, can I help you?

It's Calli Westbrook calling again, Thank you for sending the invoice

Would you mind telling me what those item codes stand for?

Actually, Ms. Westbrook my boss just informed me that the credit card company got in touch with us and that you disputed the charges

We've already put the money back on your card— so why are you wasting our time?

I just want to know what was sent

I think we're done here

Could I at least order a catalogue?

Unbelieveable...

Click

Bugger

Mergow

What's up?

You think I ought to go on a field trip?

You're probably right Watson

Hey, Theo. Could you do me a favour?

If I forward you a number, could you call and order a catalogue?

Oh, and better if you don't use the name "Westbrook"

It's a long story...

Yeah, okay. Thanks

Exotic Nailz

Hi, How can I help you?

A couple of weeks ago a package was delivered here for a "Calli Westbrook"

We get packages delivered here every day

But were you here for that one?

I don't recall

Is that your manager?

I'll ask her

Wait!

Ha, ha! Pedicure? Sure, please follow me

Wha—

I'm not comfortable—

OMG, Lady. Can you just do me a solid and play along?

Ha ha! Here we go

I'm like, a minute away from being fired by my boss slash mother

Let's get these shoes off

This feels strangely... nice

So you were here for the delivery?

Why do you want to know about that anyway?

Because whatever was sent here was bought using my credit card

Oh...

Bummer

This is so messed up

Why couldn't you let your mom know you were doing a favour for a customer

My mother is like, super hard core

Anything remotely sketchy and she's out

There! All done

Fantastic

WTF, lady!?! You have to wait until it dries!!!

I think I'll risk it

Fine. Suit yourself

Follow me to the front, I'll ring you up

I beg your pardon?

Cool your pits... it'll just be for show

Hey, Calli!

Hey, wait. Where're you going?

Back to the office

Join us for a sec. We're just waiting for food

I could try to trace that address for you. I would need you to forward me the actual email. I could copy the header into an analyzer... get an IP address from that and then do a WHOIS query

All super basic stuff. Do you have a copy of it with you?

Look at his eyes light up!

Order up for Steph

Yes, I do

Oh, sorry

I can already tell that wouldn't work

It's a gmail account. Doing anything beyond the other stuff would be...

Ummm...

Shady

I ask him to do Lisbeth Salander stuff for me all the time. Never once! Never once!

You know I'd like to...

I'm teasing

101

Chapter 8

Talk About a Stranger

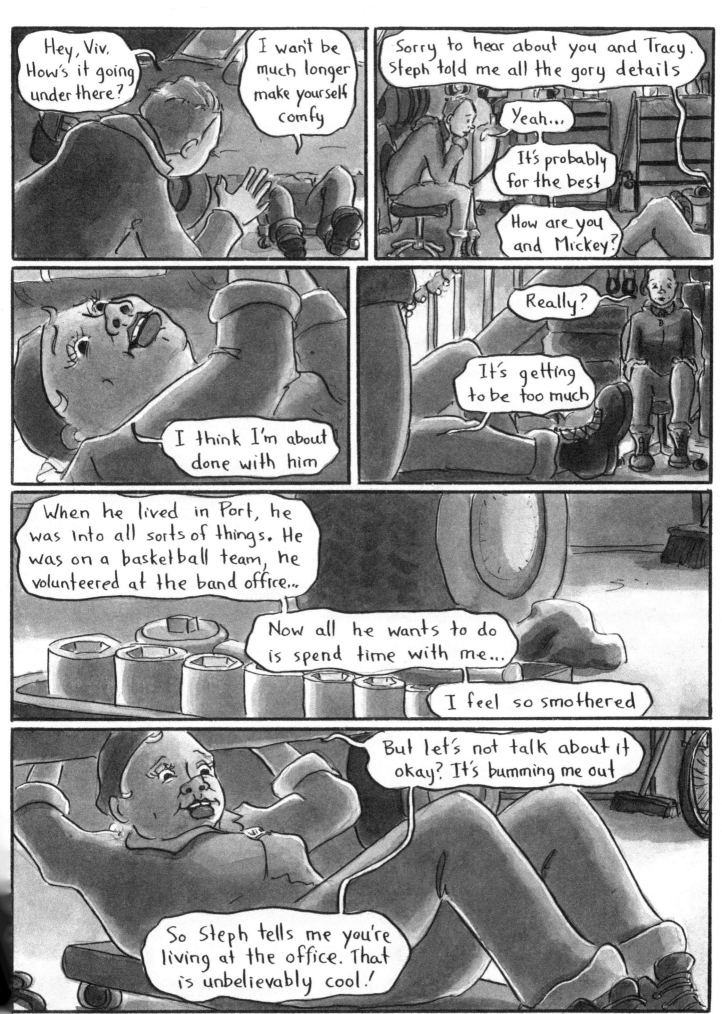

I think I'm actually starting to like it...

Mostly...

Aside from being cold all the time, having no shower or laundry and not much of a kitchen

And lately there've been a few... uh... let's say weird things happening

Like what?

Well, for instance, I've been renting out the small office to this lady, and things were going fine

But then - and I know this is gonna sound crazy-

But I think she's been abducted!

Are you effing serious?

There's a mystery to solve?

Not to make light of a serious situation but...

This is like a dream come true!

Ugh! It's the exact opposite! I'm so not cut out for this!

I'm not even sure anymore if she was taken or if she went willingly

Whoa! Slow down Warshawski. Let's go through it

And she knew exactly who I was... she was all...

Mean

Those two deserve each other

You didn't like Tracy either?

Pfffft! You are WAY too good for her

She had zero appreciation for the amazing thing you'd created

And she always called me "Val"

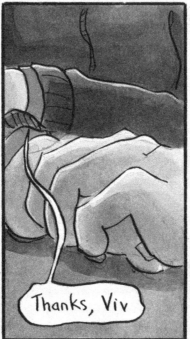

Thanks, Viv

So, back to business

And speaking of his boots, that's how I know the break-ins were done by the same guy

First break-in: boot print in snow. Second break-in: boot print in fingerprint powder

I took a page out of "The Good Detective Guide" and booby-trapped the front door

See?

And you say you're not a detective!

I think you're onto something about his expensive look

That's a Freiburg boot

They're a local company

High-end, small-scale manufacturing

That chevron is part of their logo, and also their signature tread on every sole

Only one retail outlet in Victoria

Right on Johnson

111

Hey, Buddy

I've decided something

I'm not going to doubt her

She didn't use my credit card

She didn't. She just wouldn't

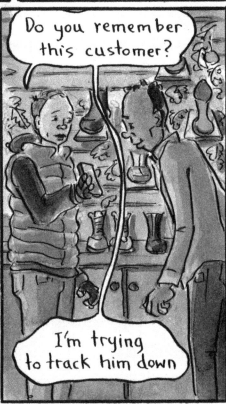

So he DOES come here

Every weekday. In fact, he should be here soon

He always comes in between 10 and 10:30

Oh, okay. In that case, could I get a small coffee?

And, would you mind not mentioning me? I'd like to surprise him

Hey, Viv. Guess what?

You found him!

Not yet, But you were right...

I'm at the place where he gets coffee every day

Oh my God! He just came in

This is so cool! I wish I was there with you

What's happening?

He's at the counter

Oh, wait – he's leaving I've gotta go!

Keep me posted!

Okay, I'll call you later

Buzz
Buzz

Hey Theo...

Hey Cal,
You got
a sec?

Um... not really,
Why?

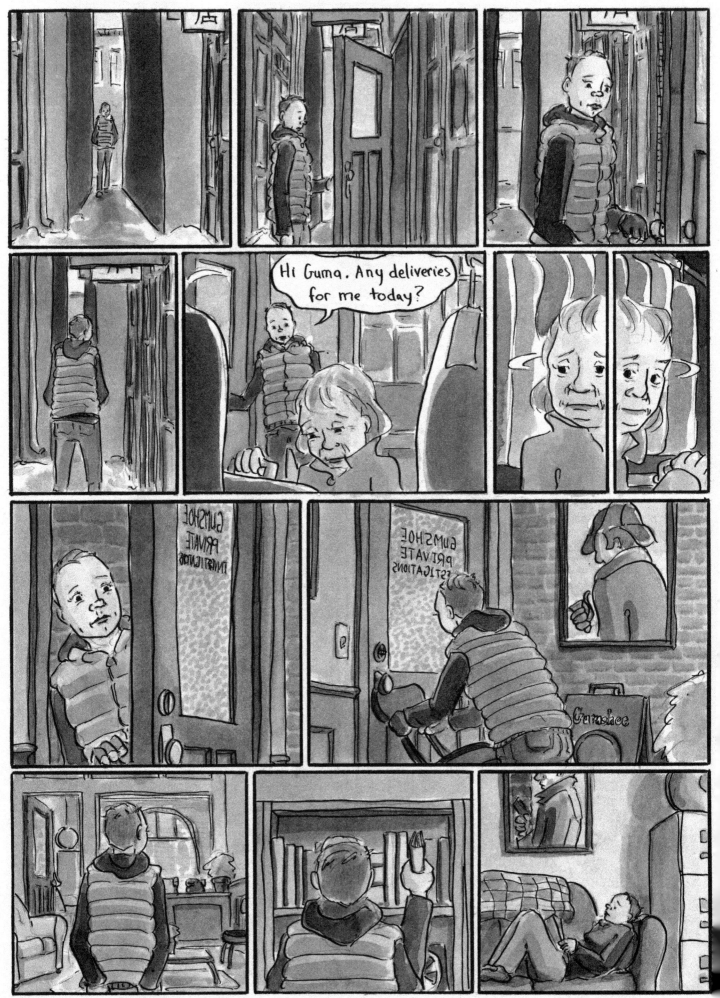

Buzz
Buzz

Hey,
Viv

How did
it go?

I totally
messed up

What
happened?

He saw
me

It's kind of soul crushing

What is?

Realizing that I'd
be a terrible P.I.

Oh Calli! Don't be so
hard on yourself! Where
are you right now?

At the
office

Um... is that
a good idea?
Why don't you
come to the garage
and debrief?

My shift at the
restaurant starts soon

And then what?

I'm crashing
at my brother's
place tonight

Good!

Be careful,
Calli

I will
be. Talk
to you
later

Hey Calli, we got a late one

You want me to make you something for when you're back?

Your usual?

Yes please

Oh yawn! Live a little

You're one to talk Mrs. sweet and sour chicken balls

What? I need the protein

Yeah, right

That should be the last one

Good, it's starting to rain hard now

If I see you again, it won't end well for you

Chapter 10

Beware, My Lovely

The greatest danger could be your stupidity

Hey! Your place is thataway. Where're you going?

To the hospital I think

Shit...

MRS. WONG!

Cape Breton, and her husband lost his job at the mine over

ing six weeks, and then we went back to Truro for the time

You're talking loud again

Am I?

Your hearing must be going again

That's the only reason people talk loud-that, or they are excited

So?

I didn't just fall off my bike... I was hit by a car...

On purpose

WHAT!?

Calli!

A lot has happened in the last few days. I think it all has to do with Ellen

Ellen? Your renter Ellen? What about her?

She's disappeared -I mean- I'm fairly certain she was taken - like, forcibly

Whoa, Whoa, whoa! Okay... start from the beginning

That's totally outrageous

I can't believe he tried to run you over!

And I was the one who introduced you to Ellen

We can't let him get away with this

We should call the cops

We know where he'll be during the day

No! Please stop!

What is it?

You don't understand

I just want to drop it and forget about all of it!

Please don't make me do anything

Oh, hey...

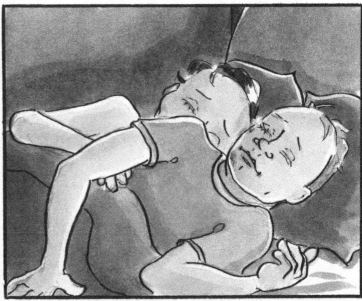

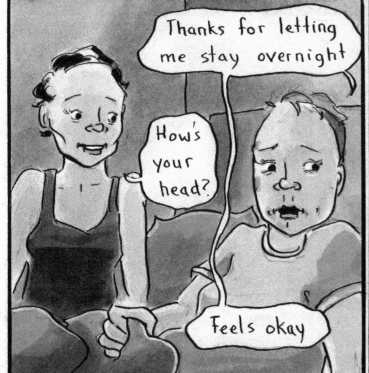

Maybe not, but

But I don't think I can stop

Rustle, Rustle, Thump!

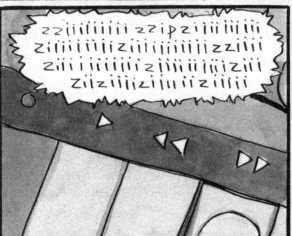

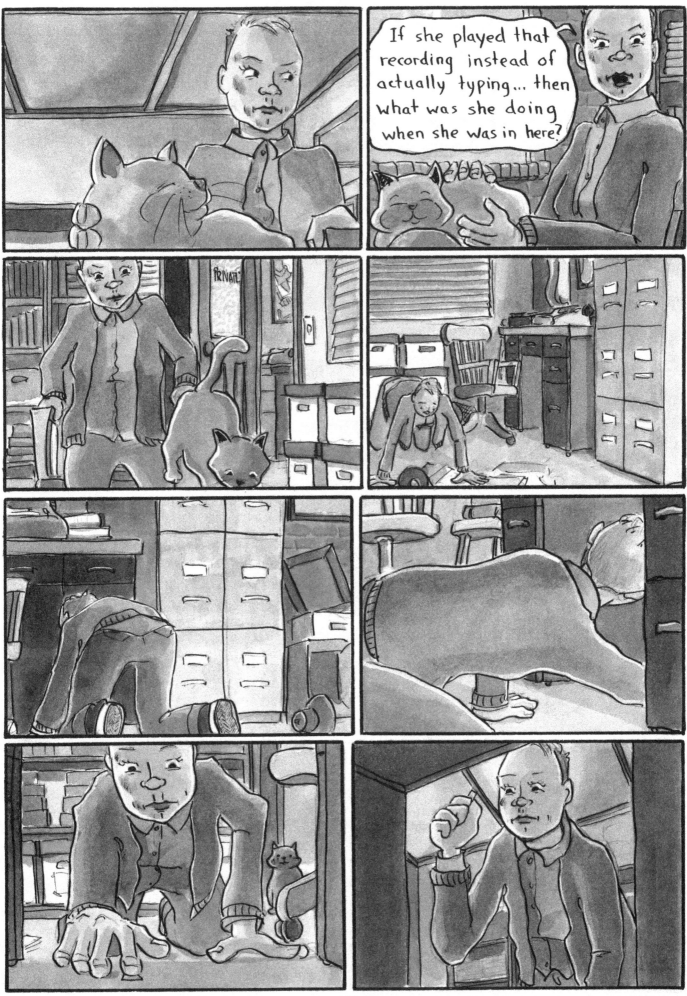

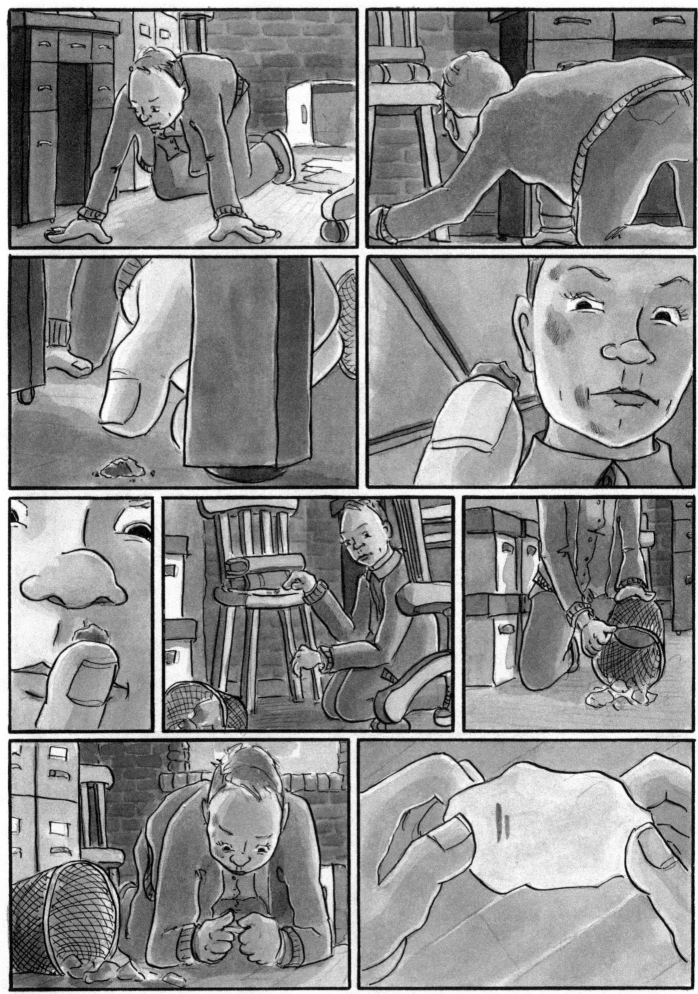

knock! Knock!

We kept your bike at the restaurant

Oh, thanks David

It's pretty wrecked

Are you okay?

I'm okay. Just a bit sore

I'll see you tomorrow

We're all at the restaurant if you need anything

Okay, thanks again

It's not worth it

155

Chapter 11

Take One False Step

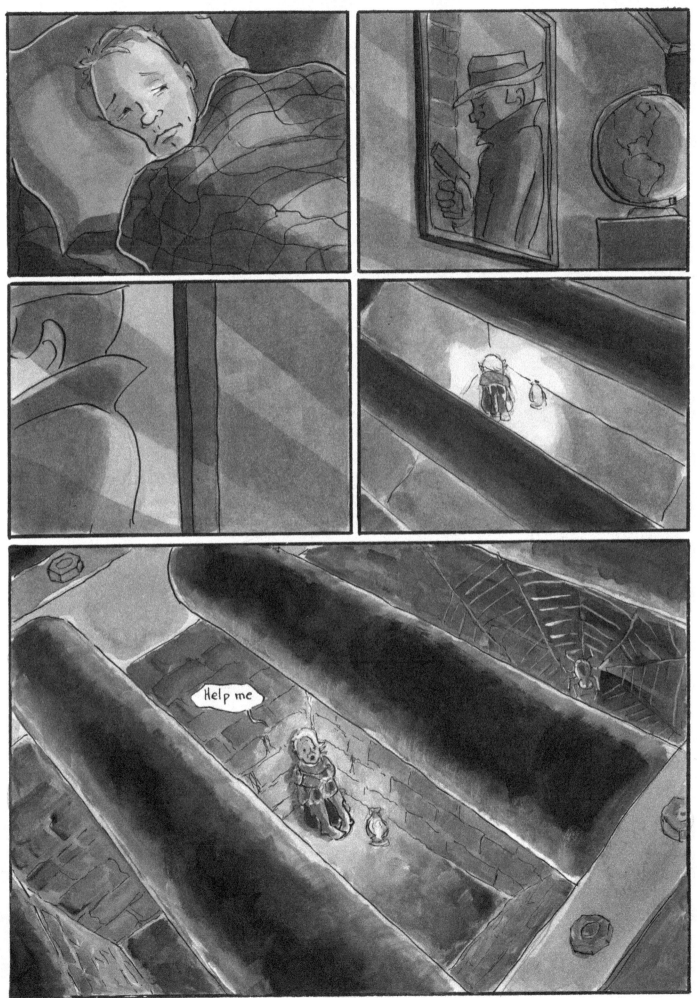

GAH!

What if I'm the only one who can help her?

Why does it have to be me?

Fuck

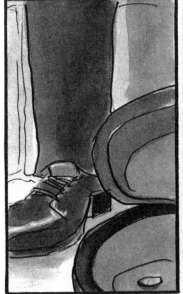

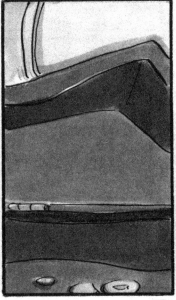

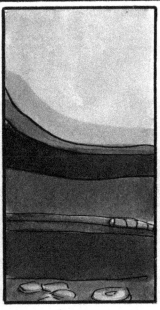

Crap

Hi, Viv

So how would you feel about joining me on a stakeout?

WHAT THE !!?

It's just me

That doesn't sound very balanced

Good for you for making that decision

I feel awful. He's such a good guy

Anyway... enough on that subject

Where were we?

Sweets, treats, anonymous 911 calls

We need to know if Calli's office-mate, Ellen, is on that yacht

Ooh, I know! Chet, why don't you run back to the office and get your toy helicopter that's rigged with a camera

You could fly that thing around the yacht and have it peek into every window or porthole

Um, yeah... nope. Not gonna happen

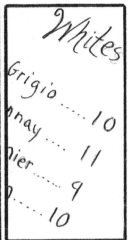

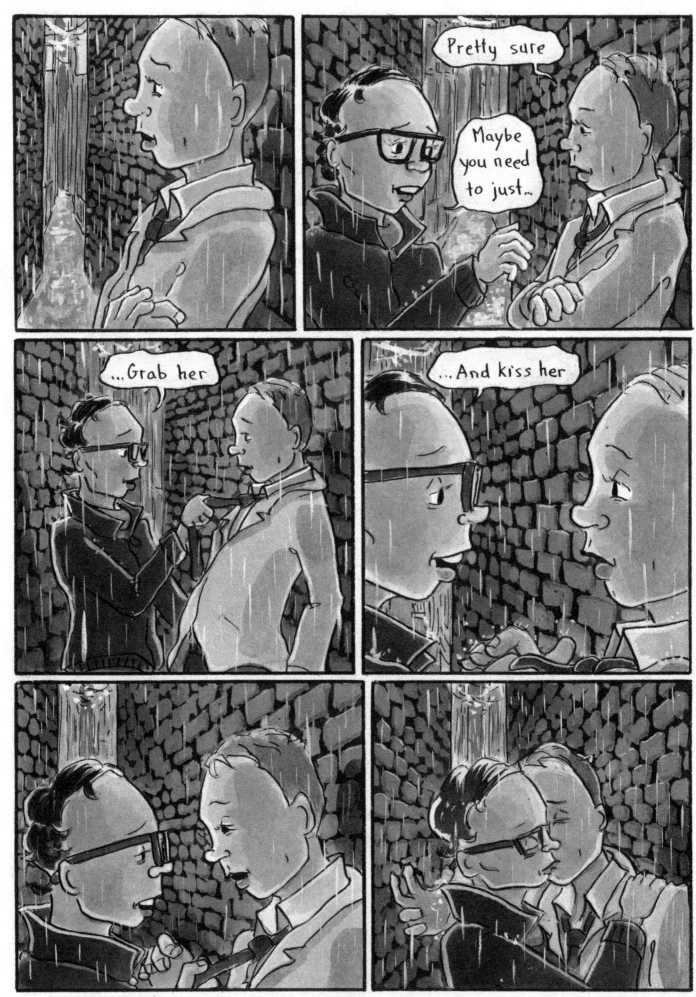

Chapter 12
Because of You

I don't get it

I don't get it

Was she just messing around like a straight girl?

Did she want my crush to be on her because it's flattering?

Or because she likes me?

She doesn't like me like that

She can't...

Could she?

I wish I hadn't drunk so much

Drank so much?

Drunk so much

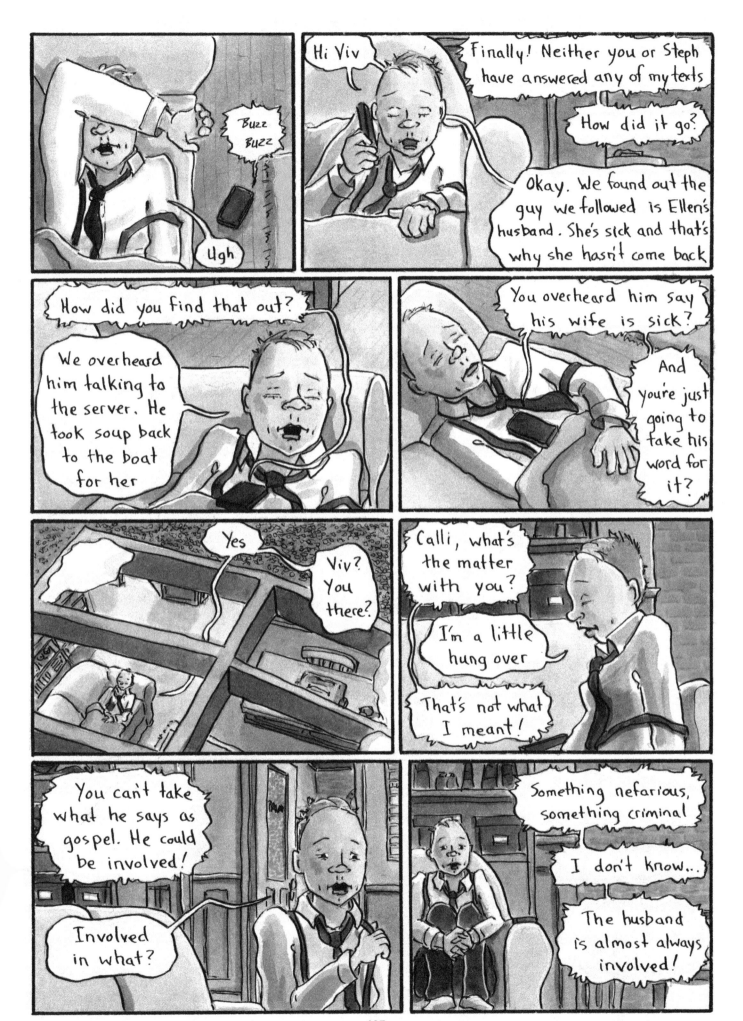

Okay I'll catch up with you later

Bye

Holy shit!

YATES

Philanthropist Elio Moretti Illuminates Victoria

TOP TEN RESTAURANTS

No wonder Steph said he looked familiar

PAPER CHASE

Philanthropist and historian Elio Moretti and his wife Helen Smith. They make the perfect team: Moretti an authority in the field of antique manuscripts and Smith an expert in preservation and restoration

That's Ellen!

Here in Victoria overseeing an exhibition of illuminated works from 1168 AD to 1736 AD... at the Museum from September 1st to November 26th

Then on to Seattle...

November 26th. That's two days from now

My name is Mr. Jigglesworth. I live nearby. My folks feed me regularly, hence my big belly

They know I'm a bit of a wanderer

Thank you for giving me a safe space to hang out in

Awww... how sweet is that?

I can feel something else

Only a secure guy like you can pull off a name like that!

AHHHG!!

What the?

Purple streaks

I can feel one more thing

Oh, wow...

Illuminated manuscripts

I'm no detective but...

These would explain the break-ins, Mr. Jigglesworth

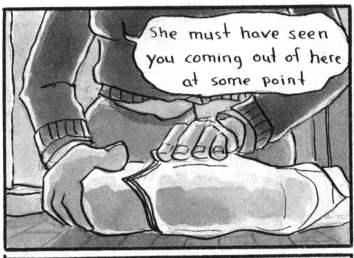

Chapter 13

Shadow of a Woman

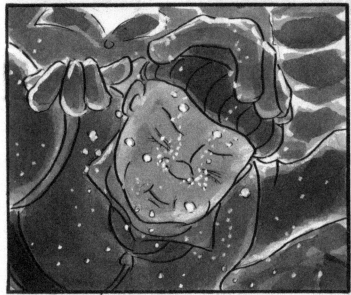
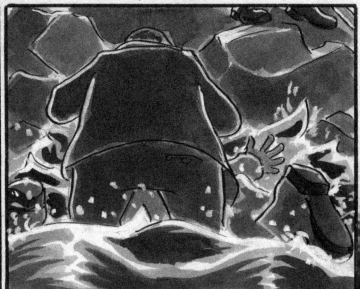

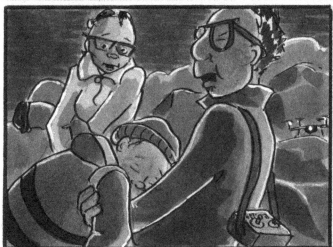

I hooked you up with the T.V.

Zoiks!

I've got to get back to the girls

Ruh-roh

And I would have gotten away with it if it hadn't been for you meddling kids!

Only $19.95! It comes with a lifetime guarantee!

A lifetime guarantee?

That's right! But wait... there's more!

Quality Curated Fine Art Supplies

If you order in the next 20 minutes we will send you—

GOLD & SILVER LEAF

Not one...

GOLD & SILVER

Oh...

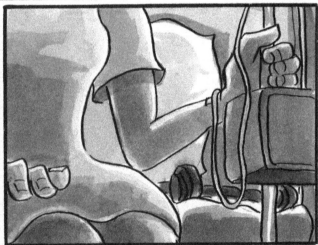

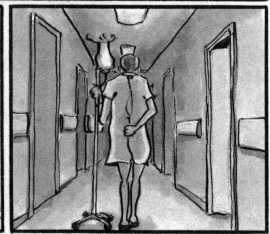

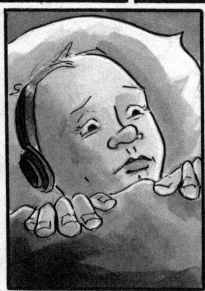

Chapter 14

I, the Jury

Oh, I thought you were still at the hospital

I just came by to leave you a note

And your key

How's your mother?

She's fine! Thankfully when the police raided the yacht, Elio didn't have time to call anyone in New York. My mom is safe, thanks to you

Elio and his nephew Mario are being held

Mario is the one who tried to...who attacked you

I'm so sorry you had to go through that

Yeah ... well...

I thought the second time he must have found what he was looking for

But then the other day Mr. Jigglesworth slipped up

Thank you

You've lost me... who on earth is Mr. Jigglesworth?

Mr. Jigglesworth is the cat's name

Oh!

I caught him coming through his trapdoor

I found your wig. I spoke to the girl at the nail salon

I know you used my credit card to buy materials for your forgery. I found gold leaf and azure blue pigment and vellum in your office

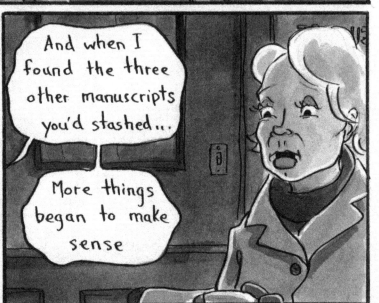

It was only three days ago that I found out your real name and some interesting stuff on the internet about your marriage

How tumultuous it is. All those affairs. You must have been sick of it

And when I found the three other manuscripts you'd stashed...

More things began to make sense

Your need for a private workspace he doesn't know about, and a few extra supplies that can't show up on any credit card bills he might see

If Elio is already getting you to make a forgery, then why not make an extra one without him knowing?

He swaps the forgery for the original, then you swap the original with the second forgery

He would have no idea

And when you eventually leave him, he's left with the fake copies

You have the originals and the most important thing...

Financial freedom

I bet, in your line of work, you have an idea of who would want to get their hands on a piece of history...

... No matter what the provenance

Your husband, or Mario, must have suspected something though

Mario followed you to this office and found you working away on a second forgery

They probably wondered if it was your first time doing that

They had to make sure

That's why Mario tossed this place... twice

Luckily, he didn't find them

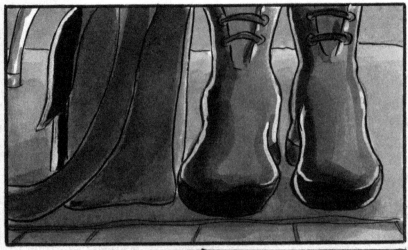

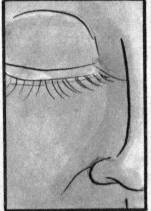

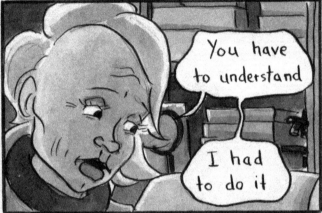

You have to understand

I had to do it

My husband is a powerful man and there would be no leaving him unless I did it right - new identity, new life, and the money to make it happen

I had no choice

I'm sure you felt you didn't

Epilogue

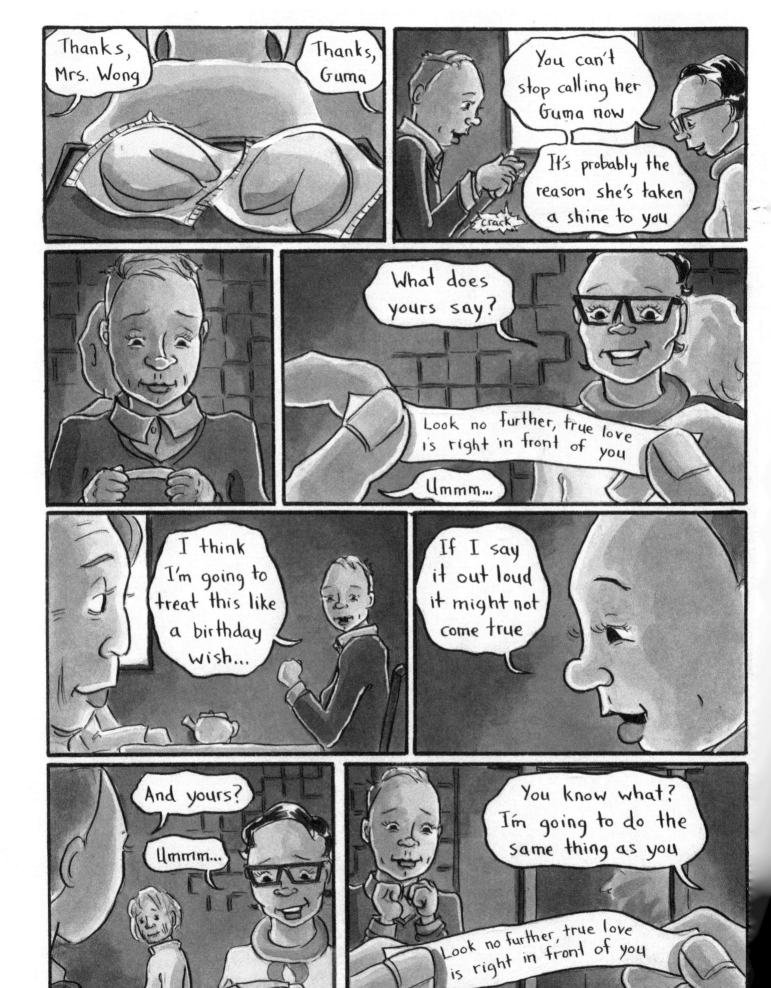

You look so much better now!

Thanks, Viv

You're looking rather dapper, Chet

It's all much less scary when it happens in a book

Whoo! It's hot in here

I have to keep mine on

I invited Mr. Jigglesworth's parents

I told them I'd wear a red scarf if they came and wanted to say hi

Mr. Jigglesworth?

The cat that hangs out at my place

You found out where he lives?

Not exactly

ABOUT THE AUTHOR

Lisa Maas is an author and illustrator who devotes her free time to her creative pursuits, except when she is bingeing Scandi noir, or falling headlong down fanfiction rabbit holes, or building elaborate structures for her cats.

Her debut graphic novel, *Forward,* was a 2019 American Library Association Stonewall Honor Book.

She lives in Esquimalt, British Columbia.

BLACK ROSE
writing™

The final approval for this literary material is granted by the author.

First printing

This is a work of fiction. Names, characters, businesses, places, events and incidents are either the products of the author's imagination or used in a fictitious manner. Any resemblance to actual persons, living or dead, or actual events is purely coincidental.

ISBN: 978-1-68513-049-7
PUBLISHED BY BLACK ROSE WRITING
www.blackrosewriting.com

Printed in the United States of America

We hope you enjoyed reading this title from:

www.blackrosewriting.com

Subscribe to our mailing list – The Rosevine – and receive FREE books, daily deals, and stay current with news about upcoming releases and our hottest authors. Scan the QR code below to sign up.

Already a subscriber? Please accept a sincere thank you for being a fan of Black Rose Writing authors.

View other Black Rose Writing titles at www.blackrosewriting.com/books and use promo code PRINT to receive a 20% discount when purchasing.

CPSIA information can be obtained
at www.ICGtesting.com
Printed in the USA
BVHW090727240722
642751BV00004B/12